THE HEIGHTS

TWISTER

SADDLEBACK
EDUCATIONAL PUBLISHING

T H E   H E I G H T S

Blizzard	River
Camp	Sail
Crash	Score
Dive	Swamp
Neptune	**Twister**

Original text by Ed Hansen
Adapted by Mary Kate Doman

SADDLEBACK
EDUCATIONAL PUBLISHING
www.sdlback.com

Copyright © 2012 by Saddleback Educational Publishing

ISBN-13: 978-1-61651-626-0
ISBN-10: 1-61651-626-7
eBook: 978-1-61247-311-6

Printed in Guangzhou, China
0611/CA21100644

16 15 14 13 12   1 2 3 4 5 6

Chapter 1

Rafael Silva sat in his home office. He thought about the e-mail he just got.

Plains, Kansas, needed a watering system. Plains had a lot of farms that needed water. Rafael had been asked to design the system.

It sounded like a hard project. He talked to Ana. They decided that Rafael should do the project.

He called the mayor of Plains. And he took the job. Then he asked about housing. He decided to rent a farmhouse.

Rafael went to talk to Ana. He wanted Antonio to come with him. It was summer break.

"He'd love that," Ana said. "Isn't that tornado country? You know how Antonio loves tornadoes!"

"I know," said Rafael. "I think he'll love it."

"Plains is near my older sister's house. Maybe Lilia could fly with you guys. She can visit Sara," said Ana.

"That's a great idea," Rafael told Ana. "I'll get plane tickets for Monday. We'll let the kids know tonight."

The kids were excited about the trip. Antonio had always wanted to go to tornado country! Lilia couldn't wait to see her aunt. *Tía* Sara always asked her to visit. But Lilia never wanted to fly alone. This was perfect.

Franco had football practice. So he couldn't go to Plains.

"Have a great time," said Franco. "Stay out of danger! You know how Dad's trips turn out!"

Antonio smiled. "I wish you were coming, Franco."

"Not a chance!" Franco said. "Not after everything you've told me about tornadoes!"

"He doesn't know *everything* about tornadoes," Lilia said.

On Monday Ana kissed Lilia on the cheek.

"Have fun!" said Ana. "And don't worry about tornadoes."

"I'll call you," Rafael said. "When we get to the rental. Promise."

They got snacks for the plane. Everyone said good-bye. Three of the Silvas were off to Kansas.

Chapter 2

The flight wasn't too bad. And their rental car was nice. But Plains was a long drive from the airport. Rafael drove. They didn't see many cars.

Antonio looked out the window. He saw nothing but flatland. Prairie land. Mostly dirt. He saw a lot of tractors.

"There's the farmhouse," Rafael said.

He pointed. Antonio and Lilia leaned forward. They looked out the window.

"It's so little!" Lilia said.

Antonio thought the house looked small too. But it was still far away. They got closer. They saw that it was big. It made the house in the Heights look small. Everyone got out of the car.

"A creek is behind the woods." He pointed. "My job is to get that water to those fields."

"That's called irrigation," Antonio said.

"You're right," his dad agreed.

Lilia looked around. "This place is creepy," she said. "There's nothing but fields."

"Corn is planted in those fields. Soon it will be tall. And everything will be green," said Rafael. "Well, only if I can make the watering system work."

"I'll help you," Antonio said "I know all about that."

Antonio and Lilia got their bags. The inside of the house was nice. The kitchen was big. There were a lot of windows. Lilia looked out. She saw fields and trees.

Lilia ran to the biggest bedroom. She put her bag on the bed. Antonio was mad. He wanted the biggest bedroom. But Lilia wasn't staying long. She was going to visit *Tía* Sara. Good! He'd move into the big room when she was gone!

Antonio's room was small. The walls were gray. There was a picture on the wall. It showed some dogs playing cards. Antonio laughed at the picture. He liked it!

Lilia and Antonio looked around the rest of the house.

"Hey, Dad, something's missing," Antonio said.

"What's that?" asked Rafael.

"A basement!" Antonio said.

Rafael smiled. "Get Lilia. Come outside with me," he said.

There was a tree outside the house. Rafael walked to it. He pointed at two doors in the ground. The doors had rusty handles.

"That's the storm shelter," Rafael said. "We go in there if a tornado is coming. After we close the doors behind us, we'll be safe."

"How do we know if a tornado is coming?" Lilia asked.

"It almost always rains hard before a tornado," said Rafael. "And sometimes there's hail. If it hails, run to the storm shelter."

"Don't worry, Dad," said Antonio. "We will!"

"What's over there?" Lilia asked. "Is that another storm shelter?"

She pointed to another strange thing on the farm.

"That's an old well," said Rafael. "It's dry now. There hasn't been water in it for years. Let's go into town now. I need to find out about my project."

They drove toward the town. Antonio looked out the back window. He looked at the farmhouse. It seemed small as they drove away. Antonio thought a twister could easily pick it up.

Chapter 3

Antonio looked upset. The town wasn't what he thought it would be.

"Is *this* it?" Antonio asked.

"Plains is a small town," said Rafael. "Towns are like cities. But they are much smaller. Most of Plains is here on Main Street."

Antonio looked up and down the street. There were no tall buildings.

A flag was outside the bank. A restaurant, store, and gas station were all painted white.

Rafael walked over to the biggest building. A sign said *City Hall*. There was a city hall in the Heights too. The people who ran the city worked there.

Lilia saw a little park. The Silvas walked there. There was a statue in the center. There were benches. And big, shady trees. An old man sat on a bench. Lilia thought it was a nice park.

The old man watched Lilia look at the trees. He smiled at her.

"Don't see too many trees on the prairie," the old man said. "They catch the breeze. It's shady here. And cool."

A girl about Antonio's age walked up to them. "Hi, Mr. Black," she said.

The old man said hello. Then the girl turned.

"My name is Jenna. Are you new in town?" the girl asked.

"Yes, but I'm only visiting," Antonio said. "I'm Antonio."

Then Jenna said hello to Lilia and Rafael.

"Nice to meet you," Lilia said.

"Will you guys be okay out here?" asked Rafael. "I need to go inside city hall. I have a meeting."

"We'll be fine," Antonio said.

"I'll watch them," said Jenna. "I've lived in Plains forever."

Antonio laughed. He and Jenna were the same age! He didn't need to be watched. But Jenna smiled at him. He wanted to frown at her. But he couldn't.

"Don't worry. They'll be all right," Mr. Black said. "I'll tell them a story about Colonel Pibb."

Rafael thanked Mr. Black. Then he went.

"Who's Colonel Pibb?" Antonio asked.

"The man on that statue," Mr. Black said. "He's a Civil War hero."

Antonio was more interested in tornadoes. So he tried to change the subject.

"I bet you've lived here a long time, Mr. Black. When was the last tornado?" Antonio asked.

"Let's see," Mr. Black said. "About three years ago. A small twister hit. It didn't do much damage."

"You haven't had a tornado in three years? You're due for one soon," Antonio said.

"Well, you might be right," Mr. Black answered. "Plains is in Tornado Alley. So maybe we *are* overdue."

"*What* alley?" asked Lilia.

"Tornado Alley... It's a nickname. We get the most tornadoes. It's part of prairie life."

Soon Rafael came out of city hall. He waved at the kids. "Are you ready to go? We need to buy some food," he said.

"Are you here to help with the irrigation?" Mr. Black asked.

"Yes, I am," Rafael said. "We're staying at the Johnson's farmhouse."

"That's a long way from town. But I can ride there," said Jenna. "I've ridden my bike further than that."

"It was nice to meet you, Jenna. Come visit some time," Rafael said.

"I'd like that," said Jenna. "I'll stop by soon."

Antonio smiled at Jenna. He wanted her to come over. It would be nice to have a friend his age.

Lilia saw something in a tree. She pointed to a metal box. Inside was a horn. She asked Mr. Black what it was.

"That?" Mr. Black said. "Our tornado siren. It's loud. It's a warning to take cover. Everybody runs for shelter."

Chapter 4

The next day Rafael took the kids to the creek. He wanted to make plans for the watering system.

Antonio and Lilia were happy to go. They ran outside. They waited for Rafael. They drove around the woods to the creek.

Soon they were looking at the water.

"It's called Bubble Creek," Rafael

said. "It's easy to see why."

Antonio knew what his father meant. Bubble Creek wasn't big. But it moved very fast. The water bubbled as it flowed.

Rafael walked around. He took notes. Antonio followed him.

"Why don't you build a canal?" Antonio said. "Like an aqueduct. That system works well. It's ancient. But we still use it today. And it's two thousands years later! It used gravity. That's what makes water run downhill."

"An aqueduct," Rafael said. "But there's a problem."

They walked to the top of the hill. Rafael pointed to the trees in the woods. They could see the fields and the farmhouse.

"This is Deacon Hill," said Rafael. "It's a good spot to build. The water would run downhill to the fields. But we'd have to cut down those trees. The mayor doesn't want to do that."

"If an aqueduct won't work," Antonio asked. "What will?"

"We'll have to use a pump," Rafael said. "So we'll need to lay pipes underground. Your idea was great. If those trees weren't there, that's what I'd do."

Rafael looked at his watch. "I have to drive Lilia to Dodge City now. *Tía* Sara is waiting," he said.

"Do I have to go?" asked Antonio.

"No. You can stay at the farm," said Rafael.

"Thanks," Antonio said.

Then Antonio smiled. He was excited to explore.

Antonio carried Lilia's bag to the car. Then he said good-bye. He waved as they drove off.

Antonio wandered around the house. He moved his stuff to the bigger bedroom. Then he looked for something else to do. At last, he found some rubber bands. Antonio grabbed them. He put them on his wrist. He was going to make a slingshot!

Outside he found a Y-shaped branch. After he attached the rubber band, the slingshot worked great. Antonio sat on the porch. He shot rocks at the trees. Then he looked up. Someone was coming up the road.

Chapter 5

Who was it? Antonio stood up to get a better look. It was Jenna. She was riding her bike. Antonio couldn't believe she came so far to see him!

"Hi, Antonio," said Jenna. "I came over to see how you guys are doing."

"Wow!" said Antonio. "I can't believe you rode your bike so far."

"It's only six miles. That's nothing! I do it all the time. Where are Lilia and your dad?" asked Jenna.

"They went to Dodge City to visit my Aunt Sara," said Antonio. "My dad will be back soon."

Jenna looked at the slingshot.

"I just made it. Do you want to try it?" Antonio asked.

"Sure," Jenna said. "I've never tried a slingshot before."

"It's not hard. Go find some rocks. I'll set up some targets," Antonio said.

For an hour they shot rocks at cans. Jenna was good. She hit the targets almost as much as Antonio.

Jenna looked at her watch. "I have to go home now," she said. "But I'll come back tomorrow if you want."

Antonio watched Jenna ride away.

He missed her already!

Antonio was hungry. He went inside. And he made lunch. When he went back outside it was raining. Then it started raining harder. The breeze turned into a strong wind. Antonio saw dark clouds coming toward the house.

He heard a loud crack. Then he heard a crashing sound. Something hit his arm hard. It was hail!

The hailstones were all different sizes. Some were small like marbles. Others were as big as eggs. A twister was coming!

Antonio ran toward the storm shelter. "Oh, no!" he thought. "A tree fell on the storm shelter doors." Antonio couldn't get inside.

For a moment, he panicked. Where could he go to escape the tornado?

Then the rain and hail just stopped. The air was very still. It was spooky.

Antonio saw a branch in the air. Then, in horror, he realized it was a whole tree. It was still far away. But it was headed right for the house. Something else was coming too. It was a tractor! But it wasn't on the ground. It was in the air!

Then he saw the tornado. It twisted and skipped across the fields. It tore up dirt and crops. The twister changed shape as it moved. It got bigger and darker!

The tornado moved closer and

closer. Now Antonio could see things in the twister's dark winds. He even saw a cow! Everything was spinning!

Antonio knew he had to stay calm. He had to find shelter. At last, he thought of something. Antonio ran to the old well. There was a rope. He unwound it. It was strong. And it held tight! Then he lowered it into the well.

Antonio slid down the rope. He held on for dear life.

Looking up, he could see a bit of sky. It got darker as the twister moved closer. It was loud. Like a giant freight train!

Antonio hoped the tornado wouldn't hit the house. And he hoped it wouldn't suck him out of the well!

He closed his eyes. And he tightly held the rope. Would it be strong enough to hold him? He didn't want to let go.

Then the twister was overhead.

Antonio could feel it pulling him out of the well! His body bounced off hard brick walls.

Antonio held the rope even tighter. He was still holding the rope when he fell.

Chapter 6

Antonio opened his eyes. He was at the bottom of the well.

He tried to stand up. But he couldn't move. His leg was stuck. Antonio was scared. But he stayed calm. He tried to think.

All the loud noises were gone. The tornado had passed!

It was dark in the well. He couldn't see much. The sky was still gray. But it looked much brighter now.

Antonio could tell that the well was very deep. He wouldn't be able to get out by himself.

Antonio touched his leg. It felt okay. He just couldn't move it. His arm was hurt too. It was bleeding. But it didn't feel broken.

Antonio had skinned his arms before. He knew it wasn't a problem. The big problem was his leg. It was stuck. He tried moving it. But it was stuck fast!

There were lots of rocks on the bottom. It gave him an idea. He could shoot pebbles out of the well. Somebody might see them. Then they'd know that he was trapped inside!

He reached into his pocket. But the slingshot wasn't there. He left it on the porch! His plan wouldn't work. He sighed.

Antonio's eyes were getting used to the dark. There wasn't much space in the well. He looked up at the sky.

Antonio shouted as loud as he could: "Help! Help! I'm trapped in the well! Is anyone there?"

But there was no answer. No one was there to hear him. Antonio never felt so alone. No one would think to look for him in the well!

Chapter 7

"I know Antonio is okay. I just know he is!" Lilia cried.

Rafael heard about the tornado on the car radio. He turned the car around. They headed back to the farm. Too late! The tornado had already passed. Rafael called 9-1-1.

Half of the house was still standing. A tractor was lying upside down in the yard. And a tree had fallen on the storm shelter! Rescue workers from Plains had just arrived. Police Chief Lopez gave them orders.

"Everyone grab that tree!" Chief Lopez yelled. "Move it aside. We need to open up the storm shelter doors!"

They opened the doors. The shelter was empty.

"I was afraid of that," Chief Lopez said. "The tree fell on the doors before Antonio got inside."

Chief Lopez turned to Rafael. Rafael looked very worried.

A rescue worker said, "It was a powerful twister! It blew down all the trees on Deacon Hill. I heard it even picked up a cow. The poor cow is gone!"

"The twister blew the roof off the church," another rescue worker said. "Luckily, it didn't hurt anyone inside."

"My son's here somewhere," Rafael cried. "We have to find him!"

"We'll find him!" Lilia said. "Don't worry, Dad. I know we will!"

But then she looked around. She saw the upside down tractor. The destroyed house. The empty storm shelter. She wasn't so sure anymore.

Antonio heard voices. But he couldn't understand them. He yelled. He yelled louder. No one heard him. The well was too deep.

Antonio had to do something. He felt around the well. Soon he found

two sticks nailed together. It looked
just like his slingshot!

He took a rubber band off his
wrist. He hoped his plan would work.

Chapter 8

Antonio's plan was simple. He
would shoot pebbles out of the well.
Someone might see them. Then
they'd know where he was. Antonio
shot the first pebble straight up. Yes!
It went over the top of the well.

He shot another pebble. Then
another. Antonio started to feel
better. Someone had to see them!

Chief Lopez had his back to

the well. The first pebble hit his shoulder. He didn't feel it.

Another pebble landed on the ground near Lilia. No one saw it. Antonio shot five more pebbles that no one saw.

"This isn't working," Antonio told himself.

Then he thought of something else. He touched a pebble to his bleeding arm. The pebble turned bright red. He put it in the slingshot. Then he sent it flying out of the well.

No one saw the red pebble either.

"I think we have to take a break here. We need to go back into town," said Chief Lopez. "A lot of other people need help too."

Rafael was mad. "You can't just

give up!" he cried.

"I'm sorry, Mr. Silva. But it'll be dark soon," Chief Lopez said. "We'd like to find Antonio. But as you can see, he's not here."

Everyone walked away.

"We can't just let them leave!" Lilia yelled. "They can't give up!"

"They already have," Rafael said. "We'll keep looking. Okay, Lilia?"

Lilia had never heard her father sound so upset.

The men climbed into their trucks. Lilia ran toward them. Then she saw something red fly past her face.

She stopped. She turned around. Something small and red landed at her feet. It was a pebble. She picked it up. And she looked at her fingers.

Her fingers were red. It was blood!

Then Lilia saw lots of pebbles on the ground. Some of them were red too. She looked around. Another red pebble flew out of the well. It landed in front of her.

"Dad, come here!" Lilia yelled. "Antonio is in the well!"

Rafael ran toward the well. Yelling. Chief Lopez and the rescue workers heard him. They ran toward the well too.

Chapter 9

Antonio saw faces looking down at him. There was his dad! There was Lilia! His idea worked!

"Are you all right?" Rafael yelled.

"I'm okay!" Antonio yelled back. "But I'm stuck! My leg is trapped!"

"We can lower you a rope. Do you think we could pull you up?" a worker shouted.

"No!" yelled Antonio. "I can't get

my leg out!"

"We'll have to lower someone down," Chief Lopez said. "Then we'll pull them up."

"But the well is narrow," a worker said. "It has to be someone small."

"I can do it!" Lilia shouted.

"Looks like he's trapped under wood," said the chief. "You won't be strong enough," he said. "That wood looks heavy." The chief shined his light on the bottom of the well.

"She can tie up the wood," said Rafael. "Lilia knows how to tie strong knots."

"Lilia, we'll lower you down. Tie some rope around the wood. We'll pull it up. Then we can lift you and Antonio out of the well," her father said.

Rafael tied rope around Lilia. Then the men lowered her into the well. They used flashlights to see the bottom.

She made it! Lilia tied a piece of rope around the wood. She looked up.

Lilia yelled, "Pull!"

The men pulled hard. The heavy wood barely moved. But that was all Antonio needed. He pulled his leg free.

"Okay!" Lilia yelled. "Antonio's leg is free!"

The rescue workers lowered the wood. This time, it was not on Antonio's leg. Everyone yelled and cheered.

Lilia untied the rope from the wood. She tied it around Antonio.

"You can pull Antonio up now!" yelled Lilia.

Antonio began to rise. Lots of hands reached down to get him. The rescue workers grabbed him. Antonio was out of the well!

They lowered the rope again. Lilia tied the rope around her waist. Soon she was out of the well. Antonio hugged Lilia. He hugged his dad.

Antonio looked around. He couldn't believe what happened. The farmhouse was destroyed.

"Using the well as shelter was a great idea," Chief Lopez said. "It saved your life!"

Antonio had never been so happy. He got to see a twister up close. And he survived!

Chapter 10

The tornado was big news. And so were Antonio and Lilia. An article in the paper told the whole story. There was even a picture.

It was a week later. Jenna and Antonio sat on the park bench. Jenna kissed Antonio on the cheek. She told him she was proud of him. Antonio was so happy.

Workers were putting a new roof

on the church. Repairs were made around town.

"Is your dad meeting with the mayor again?" Jenna asked.

"Yes. He's trying to get his plan approved," Antonio said.

Rafael walked down the steps of city hall. He was carrying some papers. He looked happy.

"Did the mayor okay your plan?" asked Antonio.

"He sure did!" Rafael said. "They're going to build on Deacon Hill. It's going to be designed just like the Roman aqueducts."

"Awesome!" Antonio explained. "I knew that old system would work."

"Let's get going," said Rafael. "We

have to pack our bags. Then pick up Lilia."

Jenna smiled at Antonio. "I'll miss you," she said. "Will you e-mail me?"

"Totally," Antonio said. "Friend me too, okay?"

"You'll see each other again," Rafael said. "Antonio will be here for the project's opening. After all, the plan was his idea!"

Everyone said good-bye. Antonio and his father drove back to the farmhouse for a last look. It was a disaster. The tornado did change a lot of things. Mostly it destroyed them. But a *few* things—it made better.